Thanksgiving Graces

ISBN-13: 978-0-8249-5634-9

Published by Ideals Children's Books
An imprint of Ideals Publications
A Guideposts Company
Nashville, Tennessee
www.idealsbooks.com

Color separations by Precision Color Graphics
Caseside and jacket printed in the USA
Text printed and bound in Mexico

Library of Congress CIP data on file

Designed by Katie Jennings

RRD-Rey_May11_1

Thanksgiving Graces

Written by Mark Kimball Moulton

Illustrated by David Wenzel

ideals children's books.

Nashville, Tennessee

The turkey's in the oven
and the dinner table's set.
The house feels warm and cozy,
though no guests have come by yet.

I'm helping Mom and Grandma
in the kitchen with the pies
when Dad bursts through the door and calls out,
"Look who's here! Surprise!"

"Charlie!" Mom and Gram exclaim.
"How wonderful! Come in!"
"You'll stay for dinner, won't you?"
Grandma asks him with a grin.

Charlie tips his hat and says,
"I will on one condition—
you'll let me wash those pots and pans
and tidy up the kitchen."

"If you insist," my grandma laughs.
"They're yours!" my mom agrees.
So Dad and I set one more place
as Mom starts on the peas.

"I'm home!" The front door opens.
It's my older brother, Jim.
He's just arrived from college
and he's brought a friend with him.

Amid our gales of greetings,
Grandpa finds another chair.
My sister bends to hug me
and then ruffles up my hair.

Jim tastes the gravy. "Yum!" he says, then lifts another lid and sticks a finger in to taste, just like a little kid.

My mother laughs, then asks if he will slice up some tomatoes, as Dad adds milk and butter to his special mashed potatoes.

Outside, a horn is beeping. To the window we all run,
to see my aunt from out of town and her adopted son.

"Looks like we'll need a few more chairs,"
says Grandpa with a wink.
"And maybe one more table is in order, come to think."

My aunt has brought fresh flowers.
Grandma finds a pretty vase,
as Dad and Grandpa rearrange
the room to make more space.

The kitchen's growing smaller
by the minute—louder too—
with everybody wishing,
"Happy Thanksgiving to you!"

The coffeepot is perking. Grandma gives the beans a stir.
The teapot whistles joyfully beside the mixer's whir.

The telephone begins to ring. "It's Bonnie!" calls my brother.
"She wants to know if she can bring her cousin and her mother."

"Of course!" my mom and dad reply. "We'd love to have them here.
We haven't seen the three of them since sometime late last year."

Our table grows and grows and grows as more and more stop by.
I peer around at everyone and catch my grandma's eye.

"What's wrong?" she asks me kindly as she sets me on her knee.
I ask her, "Will there be enough?"
She smiles. "Of course! You'll see.

"Do you recall the story of the fishes and the bread?
How Jesus made them last till all his company was fed?

"That's just the way it seems to work.
The more you love and care,
the more there always seems to be
for everyone to share.

"So run and fetch another chair
and set another place.
Then wash your hands and comb your hair.
It's almost time for grace."

She hugs me close, then rises
with a smile to help my mother
to carry in the steaming bowls
with Sister, Dad, and Brother.

There's stuffing, mashed potatoes,
turnips, gravy, rolls and beans,
yams as sweet as candy,
and a salad of mixed greens.

Then Grandpa brings the turkey in. The fragrance fills the air.
We all hold hands around the room and bow our heads in prayer.

"Thank you for the world so sweet.
Thank you for the food we eat.
Thank you for the birds that sing.
Thank you, God, for everything."

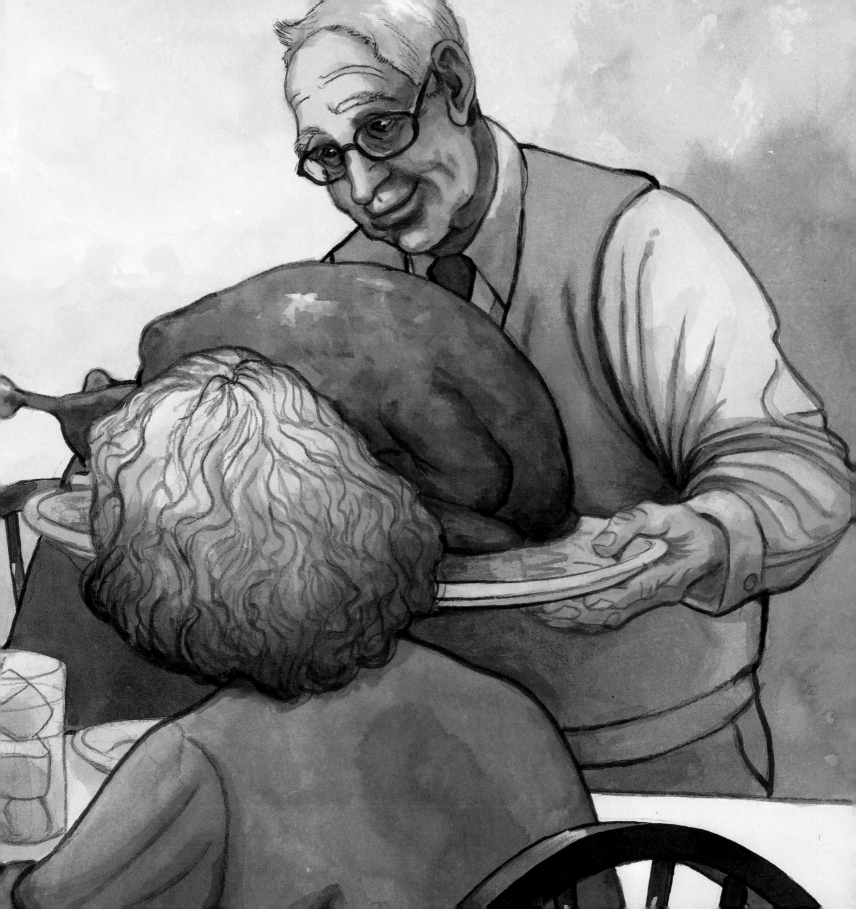

I crack an eye and peek at all our loved ones gathered here—
our friends and family, old and new, whom we hold near and dear.

I marvel at the grace my family shows to everyone.
It's something to be proud of, after all is said and done—

just like that first Thanksgiving, when the native people came
to help the Pilgrims with their gifts of corn and wild game.

And all at once I understand
what Grandma really meant,
the reason why we gather
for this annual event.

We're thanking God for all the gifts he graciously provides,
for food and health and happiness and safe, warm firesides.

And when we open up our hearts
and share these gifts with grace,
the world we live in suddenly
becomes a better place.

So come—the more the merrier!
Of this, I have no doubt—
that sharing what we have
is what Thanksgiving's all about!